First published in Belgium and Holland by Clavis Uitgeverij, Hasselt – Amsterdam, 2011
Copyright © 2011, Clavis Uitgeverij

English translation from the Dutch by Clavis Publishing Inc. New York
Copyright © 2013 for the English language edition: Clavis Publishing Inc. New York

Visit us on the web at www.clavisbooks.com

Chick's Works of Art written by Thierry Robberecht and illustrated by Loufane
Original title: *De kunstwerkjes van Kippetje*
Translated from the Dutch by Clavis Publishing

ISBN 978-1-60537-138-2

This book was printed in November 2012 at Proost, Everdongenlaan 23, 2300 Turnhout,
Belgium

First Edition
10 9 8 7 6 5 4 3 2 1

Thierry Robberecht & Loufane

Chick's
WORKS OF ART

Clavis

NEW YORK

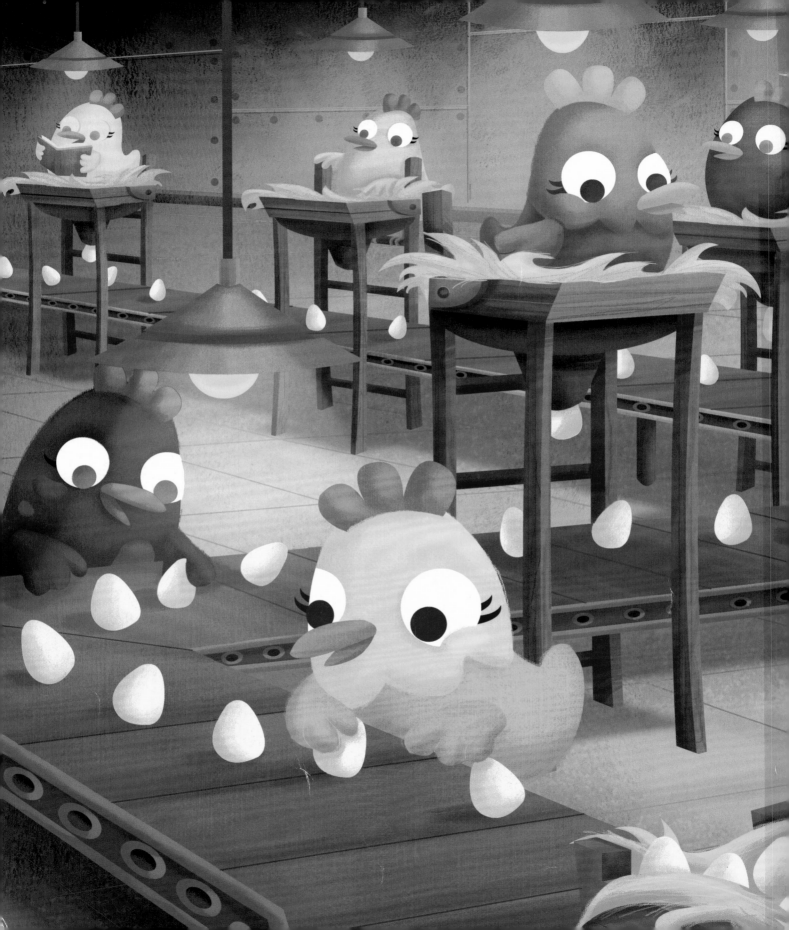

Chick works in a very big egg factory.
It's incredible how many eggs are made there!
Chick has hundreds of friends there,
as well as a couple of stern bosses.

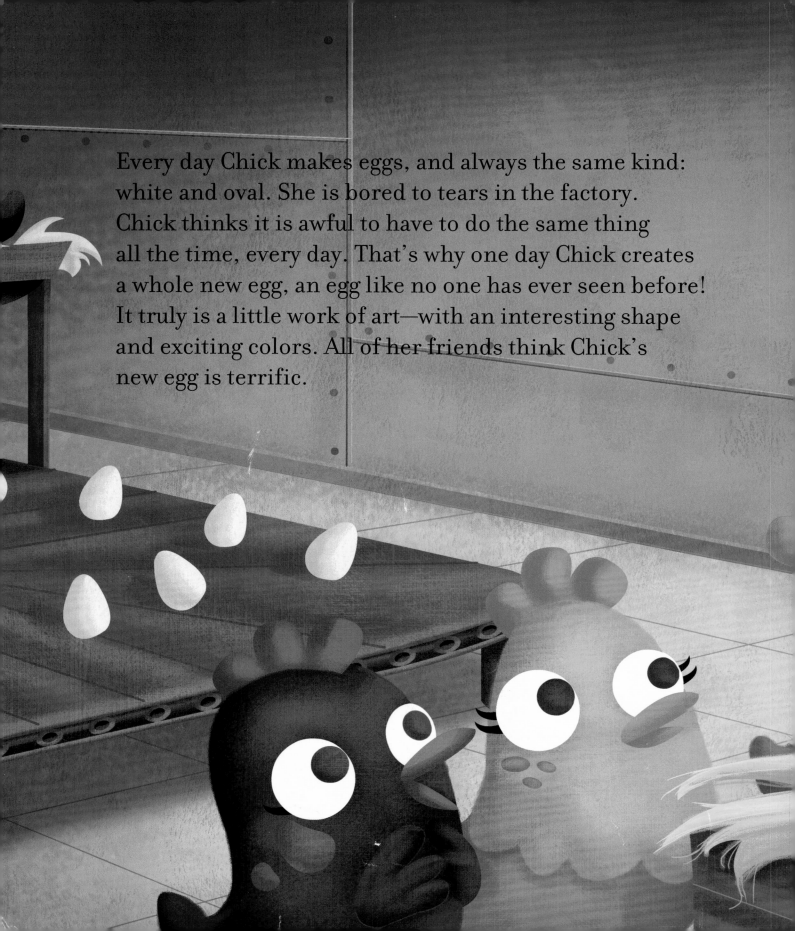

Every day Chick makes eggs, and always the same kind: white and oval. She is bored to tears in the factory. Chick thinks it is awful to have to do the same thing all the time, every day. That's why one day Chick creates a whole new egg, an egg like no one has ever seen before! It truly is a little work of art—with an interesting shape and exciting colors. All of her friends think Chick's new egg is terrific.

Too bad Chick's bosses think otherwise.
They break her egg on the ground!
Her beautiful little work of art…. "Do you think that eggs
like these will fit in our egg boxes?" they command.
"We want white oval eggs. All the same!
You understand?"

Over the next few days, Chick obediently makes regular eggs. But it's no life to do the same thing over and over again. Chick is soon bored once more and she secretly resumes making special eggs just for herself and her friends.

"Boy, you really are an artist, Chick," say her friends, all cackling with admiration.

But soon the bosses find out that Chick is making special eggs again. She immediately gets fired.
"We do not want to see you here anymore!" the bosses bark. Chick runs outside into the rain. She's lost her job and she didn't even have a chance to say goodbye to her friends!

Chick walks through the streets of the big city.
She starts to shiver and feels quite hungry,
but she is completely out of money.
And it keeps on raining.
In the evening, everybody is going home,
but Chick doesn't know where to go.

To make some money, Chick tries to sell a few of her special eggs on the street. Now and then a passerby throws her a coin and sometimes somebody wants to buy one of her eggs.
Chick feels so alone, she could cry....

And then, the next day, an exquisite lady walks by.
She stops when she sees Chick's eggs.
"Your eggs are truly beautiful," she says.
"Do you really think so?" Chick replies.
"I sell them for a dollar each."
"But they are works of art!" the lady says, shaking her head.
"You know what we'll do? You come along with me."

The lady whose name is Leonora takes Chick to her home.
And in the cozy furnished attic, Chick creates more of her
special works of art. She now designs fantastic eggs in even
prettier shapes and brighter colors than ever before.
"Bravo, Chick," cheers Leonora. "I believe
that you are now ready for your first exhibition!"

The day of the exhibition opening, Chick is so nervous.
"What if no one likes my eggs?" she wonders.
But it turns out to be a great success.
Nearly all the guests ask if Chick's
amazing eggs are for sale.
"I have never before seen something
this extraordinary," someone mumbles.
"Chick makes art with a capital A," someone else says.

And now the whole world knows about Chick's eggs.
She is a famous artist and hasn't been bored for a long time.
One morning, Leonora comes to visit her in her new studio.

"Now, Chick," she says with a smile, "show me your newest treasures."
"Well…" Chick says. "I don't really have new eggs to show you.
Lately I've been working on…a brand new project."
"Oh, really? I would love to see that then," Leonora answers excitedly.

Chick has had little peepers!
A whole brood of bright yellow baby chicks
who tumble around and around their mother.

"Here," Chick says proudly,
"are my newest and best creations."
"Oh, they are beautiful!" Leonora cries with delight.
"Yes, they are the prettiest things I've ever made,"
Chick says happily.